Fuzzy Rabb.
and the
Little Brother Problem

Rosemary Billam
Pictures by Vanessa Julian-Ottie

A Random House PICTUREBACK®

Random House 🏠 New York

First American Edition, 1988.
Text copyright © 1988 by Rosemary Billam. Illustrations copyright © 1988 by Vanessa Julian-Ottie. All rights reserved
under International and Pan-American Copyright Conventions. Published in the United States by Random
House, Inc., New York. Originally published in Great Britain as *Come on Alpaca* by William Collins Sons & Co. Ltd.,
London, in 1988. This edition is published by arrangement with William Collins Sons & Co. Ltd.

Library of Congress Cataloging-in-Publication Data:
Billam, Rosemary. Fuzzy rabbit and the little brother problem. (A Random House pictureback)
SUMMARY: Both Ellen and her toy rabbit try to avoid Ellen's rambunctious baby brother, Robert.
[1. Rabbits—Fiction. 2. Toys—Fiction. 3. Brothers and sisters—Fiction] I. Julian-Ottie, Vanessa, ill. II. Title.
PZ7.B494Co   1988   [E]   88-4363   ISBN: 0-394-80261-6 (pbk.); 0-394-90261-0 (lib. bdg.)

Manufactured in the United States of America 1 2 3 4 5 6 7 8 9 0

Fuzzy Rabbit was not very fond of Ellen's baby brother, Robert. Ever since Robert could crawl, he had grabbed Fuzzy whenever he could and squeezed him tight. Now that Robert could walk, life was even more difficult. Fuzzy would hide whenever he saw Robert coming.

When Ellen wasn't there to look after him, Fuzzy burrowed down to the bottom of the toy box and hid. But now Robert was strong enough to pull everything out and find him.

"Come on, Fuzzy" were words that Fuzzy Rabbit began to dread. They meant that Robert wanted to play, and Fuzzy did not enjoy playing with Robert.

"Leave him alone, Robert. He doesn't like it. I've told you before," Ellen said when Robert tried to feed Fuzzy Rabbit. "He's not hungry."

Ellen had to wipe up the mess Robert made with the food. "You've got your own toys. Fuzzy is mine," she said.

One day Ellen's friend Mary came over. "It must be fun to have a little brother," she said. "I wish I had one."

"I like him best when he's asleep," said Ellen.

"So do I," thought Fuzzy.

Ellen and Mary decided to play dominoes. Robert wanted to play too.

"No," said Ellen. "You don't know how. Go away."

Robert walked around the room, looking for something to play with.

"Don't touch my dollhouse, Robert," said Ellen. "You'll break something."

Ellen and Mary tried to concentrate on their game, but it was very difficult.

Ellen found a box full of toy cars for Robert, but he started to throw them across the room. It was impossible to play with Robert around.

"I know," said Mary. "Why don't you take Fuzzy for a walk?"
Robert smiled.
"That's a good idea," said Ellen.
Fuzzy Rabbit didn't agree. He thought it was a terrible idea.

"Be a good bunny and play with Robert for a while," said Ellen as she took Fuzzy Rabbit down from the shelf.

"Look after him, won't you?" she said to Robert. "Take him for a nice long walk in the garden."

"Come on, Fuzzy," said Robert as he took hold of Fuzzy Rabbit's paw. He couldn't believe his luck.

"That's it," said Ellen. "Help him walk." Ouch! Fuzzy Rabbit stubbed his toe.

"I hate Robert," thought Fuzzy. "I wish he'd go back to the hospital where he came from."

Robert picked Fuzzy Rabbit up, but instead of carrying him downstairs, he put him on the banister.

"I don't like this at all," thought Fuzzy Rabbit as he slid down, out of control.

Robert took Fuzzy Rabbit out into the garden. His mother
was talking to Mary's mother on the patio. Robert and Fuzzy
went to the flower bed.

"Look, Fuzzy. Flowers!" said Robert. Fuzzy Rabbit knew they
were flowers. He had helped Ellen plant the seeds.

Robert bent close to the flowers and started to pull the petals off. Fuzzy Rabbit was horrified. Robert's mother hurried over.

"No, Robert. You're not to pick the flowers. Why don't you give Fuzzy a ride on the swing? He'd like that."

"Oh no, I wouldn't," thought Fuzzy. It was hard work keeping Robert busy and happy, especially when people kept giving him ideas. Fuzzy felt sure the girls would have finished their game by now, and he wanted to go indoors.

But Robert sat Fuzzy Rabbit on the swing and gave him a push. The swing jerked forward and lurched from side to side. Fuzzy clung on.

When would Ellen come to rescue him? The cat from next door sat on the fence and watched, her head tilted to one side.

Suddenly Robert whisked Fuzzy off the swing and took him straight to the vegetable patch at the end of the garden.

Fuzzy Rabbit didn't know what game they were playing when Robert started crawling behind the beans next to the lettuce.

By now Ellen and Mary had finished their game and had come out on the patio for a drink.

"Dinkie," said Robert when he saw them. He ran off, leaving Fuzzy on the ground beside the lettuce, near a tiny greenhouse that wasn't used anymore.

"Where's Fuzzy, Robert?" asked Ellen.
Robert pointed at the garden.
"We'll get him after our snack," said Ellen.

Fuzzy Rabbit peeked through heads of lettuce in the vegetable patch and saw the small greenhouse. There was a pane of glass missing, so Fuzzy crawled inside and made himself comfortable. He sat behind the muddiest part of the glass and hoped that Robert wouldn't find him. Fuzzy wanted to stay in his own little house for a while. He might tell Ellen about it later.

After Mary went home, Ellen took Robert into the garden. She couldn't find Fuzzy anywhere, and Robert wasn't any help. She looked and looked, but there was no sign of him.

Ellen wished she hadn't asked Robert to take Fuzzy Rabbit for a walk. She kept searching until it started to rain.

Fuzzy listened happily to the rain drumming on the greenhouse roof and felt quite at home. It would be a wonderful place to live. At night he would have a lovely view of the stars as he lay on his mattress of weeds. He beckoned to the cat to come in out of the rain, and she jumped down from the fence. It was nice to have visitors.

Meanwhile Ellen was staring out the window at the wet garden. Where was Fuzzy Rabbit? When Robert was ready for bed, she gave him an old panda to cuddle.

As soon as the rain had stopped, Ellen went outside for one last look. She looked behind the tomatoes and inside some flowerpots. Then she saw the cat running away from the old greenhouse. She bent down, and there, sitting inside, safe and dry, was Fuzzy Rabbit. He looked a bit sheepish.

"So that's where you were hiding!" said Ellen. "I couldn't find you anywhere." She looked through the opening and considered the situation.

"You know, Fuzzy, this makes quite a good little summerhouse. All you need is a rug, and a cup to collect rainwater in case you get thirsty, and maybe a clock from the dollhouse. And if you had a notebook and pencil, you could keep a diary.

"Come on, Fuzzy," said Ellen as she lifted him up. "It's time to go in. We'll collect everything you need to make your house cozy. Then, whenever Robert is bothering you, you can stay here. And nobody will know where you are but me."

Fuzzy Rabbit sighed happily. He might even like playing with Robert now—every once in a while.